The Thirsty
Penguin

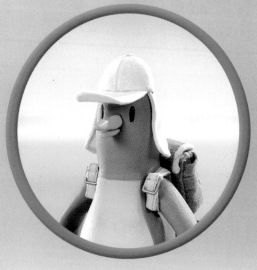

Ladybird

The outback is a very hot place – especially when you're a tired little penguin who's been walking all day! But a nice, ice-cold drink isn't always easy to find in the middle of nowhere. The thirsty penguin looked at her empty water flask and sighed.

Suddenly, she heard something. It was the Koala Brothers' plane, flying high overhead! Frank and Buster were out on their daily patrol, looking for anyone who might need their help.

But today, *they* had a problem . . .

"Did you put fuel in the plane this morning, Buster?" asked Frank.

"No," Buster replied.

"Neither did I," Frank shouted. The plane made a spluttering noise. The motor gurgled and grumbled and popped – then stopped altogether! The little plane began to slowly descend towards the ground.

Frank managed to land safely, and found the empty petrol can. "We'll just have to walk back home and get some more fuel," he said, looking all around. "Oh dear. Which way is the way back?"

"I don't know," said Buster a little nervously. "From the air it's easy to see, but everything looks different from down here!"

The Koala Brothers were lost.

Frank and Buster were so busy
thinking about how to get home
that they didn't hear the little
penguin come up behind them.

"Squeak!" she said, making the
Koala Brothers jump in surprise!

"Who are you?" asked Buster.

"Squeak!" went the little penguin.

"Do you need some help?" Frank
asked kindly.

The little penguin nodded and shook her empty water flask. "You want something to drink?" he guessed. She nodded. "And to eat?" The little penguin hopped about and flapped her flippers in great excitement.

"We're here to help!" said Frank.

But then Buster remembered something. "Or we *would* be, if only we weren't lost!" he muttered.

But luckily, the little penguin had come prepared. She pulled out a map from her rucksack and buried her beak in it. Then she flung out a flipper as if to say – *this way!* – and walked off.

Frank and Buster followed her across the wide-open outback for what felt like miles – until something very welcome gradually came into view.

"It's the homestead!" cried Frank happily. The little penguin had led them right back home!

Frank beamed at their clever new friend. "Now, let's get you a nice cold drink and some food."

"Squeak!" The little penguin nodded happily.

Buster made the little penguin a drink and took it out to her. But what could they give her to eat? What kind of animal was she?

The Koala Brothers looked in
their animal book. No one in the
outback had ever seen a penguin
before!

Just then, there was a sound of
flip-flops as Mitzi came over to
see what was happening.

"Ooooh," she cried. "Who's that?
What's her name? Where did she
come from?"

"Squeak!" said the little penguin.

"We don't know, Mitzi," said Frank.

Mitzi looked closely. "I think she's a duck!" she said. "Look! Those are duck feet! I know duck feet when I see them!"

Frank shook his head. "She's not a duck, Mitzi." He turned to their new friend, and looked back at the book. "Aha! I think I've found you." He smiled. "You're a penguin!"

Frank pointed to the picture, and the little penguin nodded. The Koala Brothers shook her flipper to say hello properly.

"Hmmmph!" muttered Mitzi, "I still say she's a duck! Ned thinks she's a duck too, don't you Ned?"

Then she walked off in a huff.
Mitzi hated to be wrong!

Frank studied the page on penguins
in his book very closely. "It says
here that penguins like to eat fish."

The little penguin nodded her
head up and down very quickly,
so Buster opened a tin of sardines.
They were gobbled up in seconds.
She was obviously very hungry!

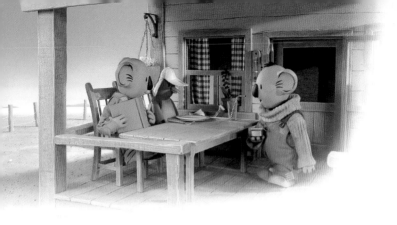

"If all she eats is fish," said Frank, "we're going to have get some more. And pretty quickly!"

So they decided to go fishing at the waterhole. Frank and Buster lent the little penguin a fishing rod. And, after a little practice, she caught fish after fish after fish!

The Koala Brothers watched, amazed. They realised that the little penguin could catch as much food as she wanted!

It had been a very long day, and
the little penguin was ready for
bed. Buster and Frank wondered
where she would sleep, but they
needn't have worried. She unpacked
a sleeping bag and pillow from her
rucksack and laid them neatly on
the floor, before changing into a
spotty nightshirt and cap.

The Koala Brothers watched as the little penguin took an empty hot water bottle – and filled it with *ice*! A hot water bottle's no good for a penguin – a penguin needs a *cold* water bottle.

"I hope she stays for ever!" whispered Buster to Frank.

But the little penguin couldn't stay.
She was only visiting the outback,
and soon she had to be on her way.

The next morning, she packed her
things away in her rucksack, filled
up her water flask, and got ready
to continue her travels across the
outback. But before she left, there
was something she wanted.

"Squeak!" said the little penguin. She wanted a picture of her new friends.

Ned and Mitzi arrived. "I didn't know the *duck* was still here," Mitzi said. But when she realised that the little penguin wanted to take *her* picture too, even she decided that perhaps the Koala Brothers' new friend wasn't so bad after all!

After the new friends had taken lots
of pictures of each other, the little
penguin put away her camera.
Suddenly, Ned remembered
something. "Where's the plane?"
he gasped.

"The plane!" groaned Frank and
Buster. It was still in the middle
of the outback with no fuel!

Frank grabbed the petrol can.

"But which is the way back?" he wondered. Frank and Buster didn't have a clue how to find the plane! How could they hope to find their way back to it?

But the little penguin came to the rescue once again. She took out her map and set off in the direction of the plane – then led the Koala Brothers all the way there!

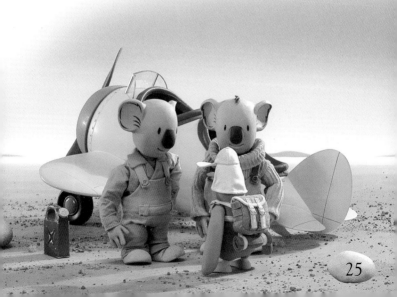

"Thanks for finding our plane!"
Frank beamed. "Now we can get
back to helping everyone again."

Buster grinned. "This time, *she* helped *us*! Goodbye little penguin!"

"Squeak-Squeak!" called the little penguin, waving her flipper in farewell. Frank and Buster waved until the little penguin was out of sight. Then they filled up their plane with petrol and flew back home. They'd learned that everyone needed help sometimes – even the Koala Brothers!

Some time later, George the turtle postman delivered a letter to Frank and Buster. "It's from Antarctica!" said George to Buster.

Buster rushed inside to show Frank. "It's from our little penguin friend! It says her name is Penny," said Frank happily.

Mitzi and Ned came to look. Penny had sent the photos she'd taken.

"I hope she'll come back and visit us soon," said Buster.

"Me too," said Mitzi, to everyone's surprise. "I'm really going to miss that duck!"

The General Store

Alice's House

Post Office

The Post Box